SPORE ATTIC

A Short Story
By
Judith Sonnet

Copyright Judith Sonnet @ 2024
ISBN: 9798337803081
Imprint: Independently published
No part of this book may be reprinted without written permission from the author, unless in part for review purposes.
All names, locations, and events are fictional (or used fictitiously).
Cover art by Terry Miller
Edited by Lucas Mangum

SPORE ATTIC

For

Chuck Nasty

The King of Stoner-Gore

and a definite inspiration for the following story.

"Almost nobody dances sober, unless they happen to be insane."

H.P. Lovecraft

The house smelled of mold and festering fruit. Stepping into it was like opening a trash can on a hot day.

His first—and last—week there, he invited us all over for a party. I showed up early, bringing along with me a pack of weed and a small bottle of pills.

I'd recently cultivated an interest in raves thanks to a fling with an EDM DJ who'd taken me to a three-day festival in the desert that summer. It'd been the most fun I'd had since I went to Disney when I was eight, and I didn't want the fun to stop.

So, I was taking lots of party drugs wherever I went, along with glowsticks.

I wore a tube top and a pair of skin-tight shorts. The exact same outfit I'd donned during the festival.

I carpooled with my bestie, Miranda. When we arrived at the house, I was stunned by its size.

Roger had sent us plenty of pictures of the place in our group chat, but I hadn't actually inspected the photos. I just glanced at them before sending thumbs-up emojis.

"Whoa," Miranda said from behind the steering wheel.

"You can say that again," I said.

"This is . . . whoa."

Miranda had been my best friend since high school. Like me, she was a party-hound, although she had a more alternative look. While I was showing as much skin as possible, she wore a too-large flannel and a beanie. While I was taking uppers, Miranda was slamming back shots.

Her head was shaved, dusted with light blond fuzz, and her lower lip was thrice pierced. In contrast, my hair was brown and messy, and I liked to tie it up.

I crawled out of the passenger seat, relieved to stretch my legs. Roger had lied in the invitations, promising us the drive from town to his new home was short and sweet.

It was anything but.

The road curved and spun through the hills, burying us deep into the Ozarks. We'd been rumbling over ditches, gorges, and body-rocking terrain for the last hour, hoping and praying that the GPS would announce that the next turn would be our last.

If we get wasted, we'll have to spend the night, I thought. *There's no way an Uber would come all the way out here to pick any of us up!*

Thankfully, it looked like we wouldn't be desperate for space.

The house was big.

Not a mansion, but close enough.

The house was three stories tall, with shuttered windows and a roofed porch. Screens protected the porch from mosquitos, which I saw was a smart move. There was a soggy, mossy pond in the front yard, and a dust cloud of mosquitos and gnats swarmed around it. Realizing my bare skin made me an easy target, I didn't waste any more time observing the house's exterior. I bolted toward the porch, Miranda close behind.

We'd known Roger since high school, but we hadn't shared any classes with him. Still, he swam in the same circles because Roger knew where to get drugs. It was, to be precise, his singular attribute. If there were apothecaries for hallucinogenic substances, Roger would be a small business owner. As it was, he was a layabout junkie . . . but at least he wasn't a *lonely* layabout junkie.

"Miranda! Chase! Good ta see ya!" Roger was a round boy with bright red hair.

"Hey, Rog!" Miranda said. "Anyone else here yet?"

"Not yet . . . but Gwen said she's on her way."

"Is she bringing that *guy* with her again?" Miranda rolled her eyes. She always hated Gwen's boyfriends—sometimes to an irrational degree.

Roger shrugged. "I told her he's invited. This one's nice, Miranda, come on!"

"She's got the worst taste!" Miranda complained.

"Hey, give us the grand tour!" I said.

"Oh! Duh!" Roger barked. He stepped aside and let us into the house. I immediately wrinkled my nose. The whole place smelled sweaty and tart. Roger caught my expression and chuckled. "Yeah, I sprayed some Axe around, but nothing will cover that scent up."

"What is it?"

"I dunno. My uncle was an old man when he died. Old people kind of smell that way, don't they? Sort of like . . . fruit. But not the kind of fruit you'd wanna eat." He scratched the back of his head. "Hey, I've already started smokin'. Y'all wanna smoke up before the tour?"

"Nah. I'll wait until the party starts," Miranda said.

"I'm down," I offered.

"Sweet." He pulled a joint from behind his ear with a magician's fluidity. "Spark me?"

I didn't have pockets, so I held up my empty hands.

"Fine," Roger huffed before taking his own lighter out of his pocket. He hit it several times before the light flared. He took a long toke, stoking the joint to a crisp sizzle. He passed it over to me before exhaling.

Roger always had the best weed. He was very closeted when it came to his sources. Some of us theorized that he grew it himself, while others supposed he had a connection in California. A few of us even worried that he was lacing his weed with something . . . more potent.

I didn't care *what* was in it. It was *good shit*, plain and simple.

I took my first toke, almost coughing on the plumes of smoke that doused my throat and curled over my tongue. I held it in as long as I could before opening my mouth and allowing the smoke to seep out between my teeth.

We walked into the living room together, passing the torch back and forth between the two of us while Miranda watched. After only a few puffs, I was starting to feel like I was swimming.

"The whole place has already been furnished. I mean, the house was left to us as is. Nothing was auctioned off. These are all my uncle's—" Roger indicated the old furniture. "All these books are his too," Roger said as he drew our attention toward a shelf on the wall across from the entrance. The shelf was tall and ornate, with gargoyle bookends. All the books were massive tomes, with title-less spines and leather skin.

"Whoa," Miranda repeated. "What are these? Pornos?"

"Ha! I looked. Uncle didn't have any deep dark secrets that I've found. Not the sexual kind, I mean. But these books are neat. It's all about botany and stuff. Rare flowers. Potent buds."

"No way. Your uncle was a pothead?"

"I think he just liked flowers and shit. But I opened this one here and . . . lemme show you—" He pulled a book off the shelf and turned it over in his hands. The book was blanketed with dust, and he'd dog-eared the page he wanted us to see. The paper looked as thin as a spiderweb, and watching Roger handle it so roughly gave me a surprising start.

"Here, read this," he said as he passed the book over to me.

The root of the Golton Fungi is known to contain healing properties if dried and smoked, although side effects include vivid hallucinations akin to Biblical prophecy, which is precisely why Golton misuse has become more frequent in fringe cults—

"Weird," I said. "I've never heard of that before."

"That's the thing. I think this book is the *only* place where this fungus has been, like, documented. It's nowhere online." Roger flipped through the pages. "Most every plant in here is either rare, obscure, or extinct!"

"That's pretty neat, I guess," Miranda said. "But what else did he leave you? Just a bunch of books and furniture? How about money?"

"He didn't leave me jack-shit," Roger said. "Mom just *gave* me the house."

"Guess she was tired of you stinkin' her place up, huh?"

I passed the joint back to Roger while he laughed.

"Seriously, you know how lucky you are to have your own place? That's crazy in this economy," I said.

"Yeah. I'm praising God. Still, it's hard getting used to the drive. I don't wanna just stay out here and be a hermit, but it takes a while to get into town. No one delivers either. Not even pizza."

"Can you even cook?" Miranda asked.

"I'm learning." Roger laughed again. "I'm learning a lot of stuff." A faraway look came over his gentle eyes.

"Were you close to your uncle?" Miranda asked.

"Actually, yeah. He came over a lot. I dunno, he was about twenty years older than my mom, so they didn't grow up together or get along that well. But he sort of took a shine to me. Taught me a lot about gardening. He taught me how to drive, believe it or not!" Roger shook his head, obviously a little hurt by the memories. "But I never came to his house. I only ever saw him at my place. My Mom described his house to me when I was a kid, and it gave me nightmares! Said it was big and dark and empty, except for him. She made it sound like a haunted castle!"

"She's not totally wrong," I said, looking around the living room. "This place is *big*."

"And empty. For now. I'm really looking forward to having a party here. It kind of creeped me out sleeping here alone the last few days. It's just so quiet!"

"And you've had no access to internet porn, you poor angel," Miranda sneered.

"Woe is me."

"Well, we brought some libations with us in the car," I added. "Wanna help me lug the beer in?"

"Sure! And I've got hard stuff in the kitchen. We're all set."

"Any food?" Miranda asked.

"I'm grillin' weenies later tonight!" Roger said.

"That's it?"

"We'll do s'mores too."

Miranda sighed. "Sounds good, I guess."

After we brought our beer in and laid our drugs on the coffee table, Miranda started making cocktails.

Austin and Jade arrived next. They were both very stoic, philosophical people, who took drugs as seriously as honor students took homework.

Austin was thin and scrawny, with a fuzzy goatee and jet-black hair greased back over his lumpy skull. Jade was two feet taller than her lover. She was athletic, black, and had long hair that swept behind her like a superhero's cape.

Soon enough, more of our friends appeared. The living room was filled with young people, all of whom had brought offerings to the party. We had an endless supply of booze and barbiturates, and things were feeling grand. Like a trashier remake of Gatsby's house parties.

Someone brought their boombox and played 90s hip-hop to set the mood. The music seemed to give the house a pulse.

Roger ran around, ensuring his guests were all having a good time. Meanwhile, Miranda was getting sloshed, Gwen and Ben were fighting on the porch, and Austin and Jade started to talk to me about mushrooms.

"It's a good trip, but it'll hurt your guts," Austin said, his voice permanently raspy. "I spent the next day on the toilet."

"TMI, darling," Jade laughed.

"Learn from my mistakes!" Austin said.

"I've done shrooms before," I said. "Mostly in micro-doses, but I really tripped out on graduation night. Remember? You were there." The truth was that I preferred MDMA to mushrooms.

"I don't even remember my senior year!" Austin said as he sipped from his bottle of homemade mead. "We did graduate, right?"

"I think so," Jade said. "It's all a blur."

"No, in all seriousness, I'm very interested in what's in Roger's attic."

I was taken aback by the statement. "What do you mean?"

"Do you even *read* the group chat, darling?" Jade asked.

"Who's got time for that?" I asked.

Austin cackled. "No, here . . . Roger sent this picture to the chat a while back." He took out his phone and showed me a highly pixilated picture. It looked like a bushel of dildos.

"What is that?" I asked after containing my giggles.

"Roger was exploring the house the other day when he finally took a gander into the attic. There's a cultivated patch of fungal growth up there. Something his uncle was working on."

"Working on?" I suddenly remembered the book Roger had shown me and Miranda, and the passage on the rare fungus, which had been "misused by fringe cults." What had it been called? Golden fungus?

No . . . *Golton.*

"Roger was talking about that. Said he was

going to show us the attic . . . but then people started arriving. What did he say? He said it was 'weird,' I think." I was struggling to keep my thoughts in order. "This is what he meant?"

I observed the picture again. Either I was too high, or the image quality was too shitty, but I couldn't make sense of what I was looking at. It looked like a clump of detached fingers, piled together like coral in the ocean. I swayed a little on my feet, feeling compelled to run upstairs and get a better look at them firsthand.

"Where's he at?" I asked, looking around the room.

Austin pocketed his phone. "I dunno. Probably smoking on the porch."

"Well, we need to get to the bottom of this," I declared. "Let's round 'em up!"

Leading the charge, I stepped onto the porch and spotted Roger sitting on a rocking chair, talking to a small group of kids who'd gathered there with a blunt.

"Roger!" I shouted. "You need to show me yer shrooms!"

One of the boys sitting on the porch looked slack-jawed. "Y'all got shrooms?"

Roger shook his head. "Goddamn, Chase! You'll start a riot!"

"I don't do shrooms!" a snooty-looking gal spoke up. "They make you *shit* yerself!"

Roger stood, leaving the blunt on his armrest. It was quickly snatched by one of the youths. He stomped over to me, looking frazzled.

"Seriously, I don't want everyone knowing about that."

"Sorry," I said with a shrug.

"Let's look at them," Jade said, stepping up to my side. "Just the four of us."

Roger looked around, as if he thought an NSA agent was hiding in the trees. I wondered if the weed was making him paranoid.

"I dunno. I didn't mention it, but . . . I get kind of a weird feeling in there," Roger said.

"Don't tell me you think it's haunted!" Austin cackled.

"No!" Roger said, a bit too defensively. "No. I just . . . you know, I got really bored the other day and—well, let's go inside. I can explain it better there."

Too stoned to really care, I followed his lead. My brain went back and forth between intense awareness and helpless complacency. I didn't even care that my tube top had slipped up, exposing my sweaty under-boob to whoever cared to look.

We weaved through the crowded foyer and went up the steps, toward Roger's bedroom. He went into the room on his own and returned with a set of keys hanging on a brass ring.

"What's that about?" Jade asked.

"My uncle had the attic locked up tight," he said as he fingered the keys. "Like, he thought someone was going to try and break in. He slept with these keys under his pillow."

"How come?"

"Because . . . the fungus in the attic . . . I think it's expensive."

"Really?" I asked. "Is it that . . . Golton thing you were telling us about."

Roger nodded.

He led us down the hall. The air around us was moist and dank, and the walls looked as if they were besmirched with dark mold. It was probably hazardous to our health, and I thought to ask Roger what had killed his uncle.

"He . . . he committed suicide," Roger intoned.

"Jesus," Austin said. "I'm sorry. That sucks."

"Thanks."

"Did he do it . . ." I realized how insensitive my question was, so I stopped asking it.

Roger answered anyways. "Yes. He killed himself in the house. I didn't want to tell y'all. Figured it'd put a damper on the party. Don't worry, he did it there." He pointed to the room at the end of the hall. "The only other room in the house with a lock on it."

He screwed a fat key into the lock and

pushed the door open. I hesitated before following him.

"This was my uncle's room," Roger said.

"Wow," Jade stated.

The room was vacant, except for a blanketless cot and a small writing desk, which was around the size of a school-table. It looked like a room for a child psychopath, locked in a mental health ward, rather than the room of an elderly man.

"How'd he do it? Austin asked, forgoing pleasantries. "I mean, did he—like—hang himself or—"

"It was an overdose."

"Oh," Jade said with a frown. "Sorry."

"My mom wasn't. I heard her talking to my dad and she said something like, 'I'm glad the little freak is dead.' I couldn't believe how hateful she sounded, man. But she *really* didn't like my uncle."

Roger strolled over to the writing desk and shuffled through some papers. Soon enough, he extracted a leatherbound journal.

"I found out why when I read his diary."

"He kept a diary?" Jade wandered over.

"What's it say?"

"Lots of odd stuff. Apparently . . . and get this . . . my uncle . . . was a *wizard.*"

We were all a little shocked by this.

"Crazy, right? But he really believed in this stuff. Listen." Roger opened the journal and cleared his throat. *"My practices have yielded only slight results, but the bud of magick does bloom upstairs, in the dank corner of my attic. For long years have I toiled, and now, at last, results! They flourish there, hidden in the dark of night and swallowed by the morning sun, allowed their elements as instructed, for you see there lay my grievous error from the first trial. Because planting the fungi in my basement left them only the dark . . . and in magick, there must be balance between the light and the wicked."*

"Sounds like something from a movie," I said.

"And look how he spelled 'magick.' It's kind of new-age, I think, with that extra 'K.' But he collected a lot of rare and old shit, and the mushrooms were—well, part of it." Roger said. "He also talks about how when his 'practices' were discovered, his parents shunned him, and his sister was so frightened of him that she refused to see him until she'd grown."

I took the journal from him and flipped through the pages.

"Here's the part you're probably wondering about. Toward the end." Roger took the book back, found the right page, then handed it over.

"The Golton Fungi haves ripened at last. I canny tell by the seeceeret song they sing me in myne dreams. Such succulance and such succulance hasey nev' been ate 'fore byy men or man—such the visions I'en eyes has seeent and seen—in forever—andever."

I shook my head. "What the fuck does any of that mean?"

"It means, he ate the mushrooms." Roger said. "Or smoked them. I think the ritual called for them to be smoked."

I turned the page. The next few were blank.

"It was the last thing he wrote." Roger took the book and snapped it closed.

"You don't think—" Jade started.

"The mushrooms didn't make him kill himself, did they?" Austin asked.

"I don't know. But it scares me," Roger said.

"Have you tried them?" Jade asked.

"No. But . . . I smelled them." Roger looked around, again as if he suspected we were being listened to. "And let me say . . . that's *enough*."

"What do you mean?" Austin asked.

"I mean that if you really, actually, truly want to get high . . . all you have to do is go into the basement and get a whiff."

"Is it safe?" Jade asked.

"Yeah. I did it a few days before I found his journal . . . before I learned that his last entry was about consuming them. I wigged out and ran to the hospital, telling them I'd accidentally inhaled rat poison. They checked me out and said I was fit as a fiddle, you know? So, the mushrooms—they won't make you kill yourself if you just . . ."

"But you don't know for sure?" I said.

"Hell, I don't even know if the mushrooms were what killed him or not. No one does. He didn't leave a note or nuthin'. And he overdosed on sleeping pills, so maybe the mushrooms didn't have anything to do with it. I just don't know for sure. I'm not going to risk it until I do."

"But how will you test it?" Austin asked. "I mean, we can't really bring potentially illegal mushrooms to the university and ask them whether they'll kill us or not."

Jade took the journal away from Roger, sat on the small bed, and began to read.

"I've been thinking about it for a while, trying to figure it out. Sometimes, I'm just so curious about them I just wanna say 'fuck it' and give 'em a try! I sniffed one the other day, and I swear to God it was the *best* trip of my life. I don't know if they're magic or not, but they are *serious!*"

"*The Golton Fungi have been used in many magickal rituals, dating back to the age before man,*" Jade read from the diary. "I've got no clue what he means by that. Magic rituals *before* man? Is he talking about, like, aliens?"

"No clue," Roger replied.

"Curiouser and curiouser." Austin chortled.

"I wouldn't ask anyone to risk it, though. I mean, we don't know *what* this Golton mushroom even is." Roger said. "But, for real, it'll blow your mind. And it doesn't fuck up your guts either!"

"I'm not sure if you're trying to warn us off this thing or sell us on it," Jade laughed.

"I don't know myself."

"What was your trip like?" I asked. "Can you describe it?"

"Sure." Roger stretched his arms over his head and shut his eyes. He breathed in deeply. "It was like having sex with God."

After hearing that, I glanced around at my friends. I could tell that they were hooked on the idea, no matter the risk. It was too tempting to ere on the side of caution. And damn it, I was right there with them.

"Should we bring some others in on this?" Jade asked.

"Nah. I don't think so. Besides, we already know how rare this thing is. I don't want anyone getting any bright ideas and pocketing 'em."

"Well, lead the way," Austin said.

Jade placed the journal back onto the

writing desk, moving graciously and respectfully, as if Roger's uncle was watching us from the shadows. It struck me suddenly that we'd been rifling through the personal thoughts of a dead man, molesting his secrets. It felt wrong, but not for long enough to stick. By the time I'd stepped out into the hall, all my worries dissipated, and I could only think of the potential high I was about to experience. The one that would apparently rock my world to the moon and back.

As a group, we followed Roger over to the stairway that led up to the attic. The stairway was narrow, and the wood-paneled walls seemed to rub our limbs like affectionate cats. We were illuminated by a single, sickly bulb which dangled from the dirty ceiling.

The stairway smelled fruitier than the rest of the house. And the air was dense with humidity. Almost tropical.

"How long does the trip last?" Jade asked.

"It's been different every time I've done it," Roger said. "The first one only lasted three hours . . . but I'll swear that I lived a lifetime in those three hours!"

I held my chest and breath as I watched Roger fumble with the keys. When the door swung open, a harsh breath of acrid air poured out of the attic and filled the stairway. I felt like I was caught in the throat of a coughing giant.

"Whoa!" Jade muttered. "That's *rank*, dude!"

"Sorry. I should've warned you, I guess. It gets pretty intense," Roger said.

"C'mon!" Austin said, situated at the rear of our party. "The suspense is killing me! Let's see these things!"

Roger walked in, then stood aside so we could join him. The attic felt like a jungle; it was humid and burning hot. I was thankful I'd dressed light and had my hair pulled back.

The mushrooms were growing beneath the far window. Each bud was like an inflatable baton, glistening with some undiscerned fluid that seemed to seep from their gaping pores. They grew on the surface of a seating area, where the window could be used as a good reading spot if someone didn't mind sitting in an unairconditioned attic.

"They're huge!" Jade marveled. "I've never seen mushrooms like that! Not in person, at least."

"Christ!' Austin pushed ahead of us and stepped toward the bushel of shrooms.

"And they're just growing out of that seat there? No dirt or anything?" I asked.

"Yep. They're growing out of the wood. That seat is actually a trunk but . . . I can't pry it open without destroying the mushrooms." Roger walked over to the wall beside the window and leaned against it, his arms crossed and his eyes wide. "So, who wants to try 'em?"

Now that I could see the mushrooms in person, I was nervous. There was something so alien about them. Uncanny. I wanted answers but knew there would be none. We'd already read everything Roger's uncle had to say about them. All we could learn now, we'd have to learn ourselves.

"I'll try them!" Jade said, stepping up to the window. She hunkered down, put her nose against one of the mushrooms, and inhaled loudly. Then, she stumbled back, wavering on her feet. Roger was quick to give her a hand and hold her steady. Her eyes seemed to swim in her skull.

"What's it like, hun?" Austin asked.

"Oh, God!" Jade said. "It hits *fast*. I n-need to sit down!"

She crumpled against Roger, who helped direct her to the floor. He propped her up against the nearby wall, then held her hand and knelt beside her.

"Tell us what you see, Jade!"

Jade smacked her lips. "I'm not seeing anything yet, but . . . I feel it. Like, the moment I breathed them in, the colors around us started to feel more . . . *real*. Does that make sense? It's like I'm seeing colors the way I did when I was a little kid!"

That sounded pleasant. There were a few highs worth chasing, I thought. The best ones made your brain feel like it did when you were a child. Before life got so hard and dull.

Jade blinked slowly, almost closing one eye at a time. "You need to try it, Austin. You'll love it."

He followed her lead. Just like with Jade, Austin almost keeled over after taking his first whiff. Roger helped him sit next to his girlfriend, then asked him what he was seeing.

"Sparkling lights. Everywhere," Austin said dreamily. He waved his hand in front of his face. "It's all on my skin . . . It feels really good on my skin—"

I was starting to get jealous. I wasn't exactly sober, as I'd spent the whole night smoking, but I wasn't nearly as stoned as Jade and Austin were.

I pushed ahead, circumventing my doubts and initial nervousness.

Approaching the mushrooms, I could hear something whispering in the attic with us. Something that sounded like wind, or like the ocean lapping at the shore. A natural, organic noise. I realized, as I got closer to the Golton stash, that the noise was emanating from—

where else?—the mushrooms themselves.

I leaned in close.

The mushrooms seemed to *throb* salaciously in front of me.

I closed my eyes and inhaled deeply.

As promised, the high hit me quick. In fact, it punched me right in the stomach, causing me to double up and squeeze my face into a grimace. It felt as if sharpened tinges had been forced up my nose.

I batted at my face, not sure if I was experiencing pain or pleasure but knowing that I was feeling *something* that was unnatural to me. Something that no human had ever felt before.

Maybe this is how Martians feel when they catch a cold. Har-har.

Roger was at my side, helping me sit down beside Austin. I could hear him speaking to me, but I had no idea what he was saying. His voice oozed out of his mouth like jelly smashed between two crumbling pieces of toast.

I opened my eyes.

I was surrounded by floating things. Little bits of shiny debris hung suspended in the air ahead of me. It looked like someone had pressed "pause" in a metal shop, catching the sparks before they died.

I hesitated, knowing that what I was seeing was a hallucination but also thinking, *This is real. You've never experienced real life before this second . . . but you're experiencing it now. This is what life will always be like now that you've opened your eyes.*

The sparks violently shifted. In the shift, I saw beyond the attic and into my own memories.

I saw myself as a child, standing outside, watching thunderclouds develop overhead. I was sad because I'd spent all day drawing portraits of my favorite cartoon characters—or were they portraits of my best friends?—on the sidewalk, and I knew the rain would wash them all away.

I must have been seven or eight, or maybe younger.

How old do you have to be before you start thinking of the future? When adults are no longer guardian angels but are just...adults? Do you start thinking that way at all when you're a child? Or do you only think that way when you become an adult? And then, do we all travel back in our sleep and implant memories of awareness into our childhoods?

I was losing it with all these answerless questions.

Back in the attic, I looked around for something that would ground me.

Jade and Austin were sitting beside me, enjoying their own trips.

Roger was talking again. I tried to parse

through his words.

Something about the mushrooms.

The mushrooms—

There'd never been a stronger drug, I decided. Nothing ever worked this fast. I was already going through an existential spiral, and I'd only been high for what had to be five minutes.

Time seemed to stretch around me.

So did space.

Suddenly, there was a whole *world* between me and Roger. In that world, there were cities, people, and animals. Strange creatures, all of them. Very unlike us earthlings. They were made of origami instead of flesh.

I wondered if they had origami sex. If they could produce origami children from their origami pussies.

I chuckled, then felt bad for thinking such dirty thoughts. I didn't used to be so filthy, did I? No. I was normal once, wasn't I? But now I was a categoric failure. A filthy animal, not even fit for human company. Not even fit to eat.

I should starve myself.

No. That's a bad thought.

Bad thoughts lead to bad trips.

Stepping over the origami people, I realized that when I lifted my foot, the ground vanished below me. When I lifted my other foot, the ground traveled with it.

One foot plunged into darkness, while the other was firmly planted on solid ground, surrounded by hungry origami people. Would they bite me if they got hungry enough?

And then I was lying flat on a hill. The grass was growing through me, which was something I'd read about in a book, wasn't it? Yes. C.S. Lewis had written about how the grass in the afterlife could puncture a spirit's feet, like the grass was made of razors.

Did that mean I was dead?

No. Only tripping.

Things were seesawing between beauty and ugliness.

The mushrooms were taking me on one hell of a journey.

I tried to close my eyes again. Behind my lids, I saw swirling colors. It reminded me of dust in the cosmos—of photos I'd seen in astrology magazines and in science textbooks.

The nebulous clouds swirled around me. The darkness around them felt deeper than ink—a pure sort of darkness that had weight and dimension. Oceanic and yawning, I fell through it, my arms swinging around my sides like propellers as I tumbled.

I tried to open my eyes, but even a slant of light was too much to bear. I kept them sealed and continued to fall, until I lost speed and began to drift weightlessly. I was surrounded now by rings, which spun about me like hula-hoops.

I'd never experienced a trip like this before. Not in all my years of partying. Never had I been so intoxicated that I believed I was taking a ride through outer space.

Or was it inner space?

The space inside me, where my soul rested.

I used to think, when I was young, that the soul was an organ like any other. That it rested between my lungs, like a meaty fruit hanging from a branch. It vibrated when I was good and shriveled up when I was bad.

Bad people had souls like cocoons inside of them. Like mothballs. Good people had shiny apples, or splitting peaches, inside their chests—

I was getting lost in my own memories again. I needed to focus on the present.

I was floating in darkness. In *the* darkness. The darkness we all experience before we're ripped from our mother's wombs and put under the sun. The darkness of pre-existence. It was not nearly as scary as I'd imagined it. Instead, it was warm, peaceful, and pleasurable.

I felt as if I was no longer Chase. I was, instead, not even a thought. I was non-existence, swimming in a sea of nothingness. And how cool the nothingness was. How kind and simple. It demanded nothing of me, only that I *not be*.

But the illusion was quickly broken . . . because I wasn't *not being*. I was *thinking . . . feeling . . . breathing . . .*

I felt hot razors fill my throat.

Wriggling around, I tried to lift my hands up. I knew that if I put my hands against my throat, the razors would leave—but I couldn't even perform this one simple task. My hands were raising up and up, but they never reached my throat. It was as if the top part of my body was stretching above my hands, just out of reach.

I imagined the highest point I could fall from. It looked like a ledge on the Grand Canyon, only this trench fell much further into the earth.

Without hesitating, I curled into a ball and tipped over the edge.

I didn't quite so much as *fall* as I did *waft* down the sheer surface of the cliff. Like an opened umbrella, I felt the air keep me from plummeting. Instead, I danced and spun and floated, falling down and down into the chasm.

I opened my eyes again. I'd forgotten they were closed, and now I was back in the attic. Roger was nowhere to be seen. Jade and Austin were still leaning against the wall. They were frozen, as if they'd looked Medusa right in the eyes.

Gradually, I felt pins and needles on my legs. I tried to roll over but realized I couldn't really *roll* while I was sitting. So, instead, like a baby, I pulled myself onto my hands and knees and decided to crawl.

But where to?

At least I had some motor controls, but I had no idea where I was going or what I was doing.

I crawled away from the wall and over toward the window, with its mushroom filled trunk. I let my fingers skitter up the wooden surface of the trunk, like spider-feet. Then, I hauled myself up to my knees so I could look directly at the mushrooms.

I inhaled, breathing in more of the tangy fragrance. I wondered why it had stung me the first time. I vaguely recalled feeling as if someone had put a hot poker up my nose. Now, the odor was simple and slight, like a pie that'd spent too long on the windowsill.

I breathed in a mouthful, feeling little specks of glowing warmth land on my tongue. Then, I tumbled onto my back. Laying on the ground, looking up at the ceiling.

My brain became pudding.

"You see, Uncle? I got three of them," Roger's voice cracked through the darkness.

"See?"

See what?

I tried to turn over, but my whole body felt heavy. I lay on the floor, seeping into it. I imagined steam rising from the earth, played in reverse, so it looked like the dirty ground was sucking the steam back into it—

I needed to be logical for a moment. Roger was saying something that sounded important.

I craned my head back and spotted him. He was standing in the corner, talking into his hands. I could see a long length of twine leading from between his cupped hands to the trunk. The twine was wrapped through the rafters overhead, and it drooled down one of the walls before slipping through the trunk's lid.

"Can you hear me, Uncle?" Roger said, speaking directly into the twine.

The mushrooms flexed, in unison. They all seemed to be breathing, but I knew that was impossible.

"The windowsill worked, Uncle," Roger said. "They're more potent than ever! I'll bet the entire party has been infected by now, they're so strong!"

Jade coughed loudly. The noise was too loud. It reverberated through the attic, making my bones feel hollow and my skin prickle. I looked toward her, wanting to plead with her so that she may never make such a horrible sound again

"Yes. It's happening now, Uncle," Roger said.

Ignoring his whisper, I crawled on my hands and knees again, ambling slowly toward Jade.

"Jade . . ." I moaned.

She coughed again. It was a wet, tearing sound that made her whole body shake.

"Jade . . . something . . . wrong," I muttered.

Jade's mouth fell open.

A mushroom grew out of the orifice.

The bulbous thing flexed ahead of her, like a lizard's tongue, then began to fatten up around its middle. It looked as if a party clown was blowing up a balloon from inside Jade's mouth.

I wanted to scream, but I couldn't. Instead, I watched in horror as more mushrooms grew out of Jade's mouth. Her cheeks split into a gruesome smile, and blood poured down her face and slicked her shoulders.

She began to writhe and judder in place, lifting her hands so I could see the mushrooms that had pushed her nails out of their beds.

I heard something *crack* inside her, like a log being split. More blood began to pour out of her, this time blotting the front of her shirt.

"She's changing, Uncle," Roger said. "Jade's the first to change. Austin will be next—"

"No!" I muttered, turning my head toward Austin. His left eye was bulging out of its socket. There was something inside his skull that was *pushing* the orb loose.

"Yes, Uncle . . . the change is happening now. You were right, Uncle. Bodies are the best farms—"

I couldn't stand what I was seeing . . . what I was hearing.

Roger was responsible for this. Roger and his sorcerer uncle. They'd trapped us, using our curiosity against us. And now . . . they were using us as *farms*—planting more Golton mushrooms inside of our bodies.

I couldn't stand it. I was so frightened, I wished I'd just go ahead and die before the pain started.

"Yes, it's happening to Austin too. I'm watching it happen now, Uncle," Roger said.

Austin's eye sloughed down his cheek, dangling by a strand of red string. Two mushrooms bloomed from the gaping socket, blood-spackled and throbbing.

My vision went fuzzy. I thought, for one painful second, that the same thing was happening to me. That fungi were crowding up behind my eyeball, desperate for air.

I lay down flat on my front, breathing harshly. I sealed my eyes shut and prayed that

I'd die before the hurting started—

"Yes. It's happened to him. To Austin. Now it'll happen to her, Uncle. Now it'll happen to Chase," Roger whispered into his hands.

"No!" I screamed from the floor. "No, you bastard!"

"She's angry. The other two . . . they didn't even notice it was happening. She's feeling it."

I hated his placid voice. I wondered if this was how zebras felt when they were being chewed up by lions, only to see a documentary crew standing a few yards away, filming their ordeal.

I rolled onto my back and set a hand over my pumping heart. It felt like there were explosions going off in my ribcage. Like someone had opened a coal mine inside of me.

Tears filled my vision.

Overhead, I could see the twine that roped through the rafters—

—leading to the trunk.

I got back on my hands and knees and started to crawl. Even as I felt something clump together inside my throat—like I'd swallowed too much bread too fast.

"Uncle, she's coming toward you!"

I didn't have to travel far. Only a few feet, and then my hands were on the lid.

"Uncle!" There was urgency now.

I tore the lid up.

Inside, I could hear the mushrooms snapping out of whatever was inside the trunk—whatever they'd grown from.

I blinked away my tears and looked in.

The corpse lay in the trunk, curled up in a fetal ball . . . covered in growing mushrooms. A length of twine snuck through his teeth, vanishing down the black barrel of his dehydrated throat. His skin was an oily glaze on his bones, and he wore nothing except for a wizard's robe. Starry patterns and bold moons swooped over the surface of his garment.

Roger's lies played through my head.

His Uncle didn't commit suicide and die in his bedroom. No, he'd used himself as a body farm, to grow these horrendous mushrooms.

I'll bet Roger's mom didn't even give him the house, like he claimed. I'll bet he inherited it directly from his uncle. The wizard, who he got along with so well—who he was now working for!

Roger grabbed my shoulders and pulled me away from the trunk. He whirled me around so I could see his cloudy, milk-white eyes. He spoke in a rasp, his voice tinged with demonic fury.

"Look at all the spores you've broken, mewling bitch!"

I threw a punch. It was too weak to do

anything.

Roger began to speak in a strange language I'd never encountered. His voice oozed out of him like smoke from a chimney.

I looked down at my hand just as my fingers bent back the wrong way. Each digit broke, sending hot spurts of blood into the air between me and Roger. Shrieking, I tried to backpedal, but Roger held onto my shoulders, locking me in place.

Aggressively, he spoke toward me. Each word was laced with acid. They were so hateful that even though I had no clue *what* he was saying, I knew what he meant.

He wanted me to die.

I held my broken hand against my chest and tried to wriggle out of his grip.

I felt three of my teeth dissolve in my mouth, like antiacid tabs in a water glass. My left eardrum popped, deafening me. My right eye began to bubble, like it had been dropped in a boiling cauldron.

Oh my God . . . I'm going to die.

He's going to kill me with magic words!

No. Not magic words . . . MAGICK words. Magick words and Magick Mushrooms and Magick Uncles and Magick—

My brain felt like it was unspooling.

I had to act quick, or else I would become a

grease stain on the attic floor.

I held up my broken hand. The skin had been degloved, exposing the red musculature beneath—

—and a hardened shaft of splintered bone.

I thrust my broken hand upward. I was thankful to hear Roger's voice cut off. Then, there came a wet gurgle.

Through my remaining eye, I squinted and saw what I'd done.

I'd speared him through the space where his jaw met his throat. The wet flesh seemed to bulge around the intrusion. Blood spilled out of his mouth, giving me a crimson sleeve.

I jerked myself free.

Roger released me and stumbled back, pawing at the wound. His eyes looked frantic, and his mouth worked around invisible spells.

I fell back onto my rump. My shredded limb hung uselessly from its socket.

I blinked slowly, my remaining eye carrying the entire burden of sight.

My tongue did some brief exploring, finding beehive like holes drilled through the roof of my mouth.

If I'd let Roger continue . . . he would've *magicked* me into nothingness.

Roger fell to his knees, then keeled forward. Face down, he gurgled once before lying still.

I needed to leave. The attic's humidity was becoming oppressive and—*please no*—I could still smell the mushrooms.

I scampered out of the attic, dragging my feet behind me.

The music still thumped in the living room. I expected it to stop once people got an eyeful of me—covered in blood, half-melted.

Instead, I found a weird stillness in the living room.

Everyone was sitting down. Some on furniture, others on the floor. The only people who weren't sitting were reclining against the walls.

Everyone was swarmed with growing mushrooms.

I couldn't tell anyone apart from each other. Everyone just looked like a soggy lump, coated in glistening Golton mushrooms.

"M-Miranda?" I asked.

None of the figures responded.

But the Golton did.

I could hear them flexing, squelching, and mashing together inside the bodies of my friends.

We've been breathing them in ever since we got here.

"Miranda? Are you there?" I tried again, my voice hurting. It was as if I had swallowed sandpaper.

Breathing them in—we've been infected—oh God—

I stumbled away from the living area and toward the porch.

Even there, I couldn't escape the horror.

The kids Roger had been smoking with were still on the porch. They were covered in vibrant mushrooms. The fungi had broken through their flesh, leaving blood-smears on the wooden floor. One naked arm stuck feebly from a pile of throbbing, pulsating mushrooms. The fingers were curled into claws, and I saw fuzzy fungi blooming in the palm, like straw in a rat's nest.

I dragged myself down the steps and onto the lawn. I knew I couldn't drive myself away from Roger's place.

My body was failing me . . .

But I knew what I needed to do.

If I could just get to my car . . . I had a lighter in the glove compartment . . . and a spare jug of gasoline in the back—

***

In hindsight, burning Roger's house wasn't a great idea.

The smoke rose into the sky above the

house, like a towering, gray pillar. Then . . . it migrated.

By the time the fire department came out to the house, the populace beyond the hills was breathing in the contaminated smoke.

From my hospital bed, I can hear people screaming.

It never ends.

The hallways are crowded with people who inhaled the smoke—who are *budding*.

I refuse to open the shades on my windows. With my one eye, I'd rather see nothing than bear witness to the hell I've created.

Besides, I can feel the mushrooms inside my throat.

I'll be dead soon anyways.

God help us . . .

All we wanted was a trip.

THE END

Extreme Horror and Splatterpunk Books by Judith Sonnet

Low Blasphemy
Torture The Sinners!
Beast of Burden
Blood and Brains
Hell: City of the Killing Dead
The Shriek-A-Rama Spook Show Experience
Magick
Psych Ward Blues

Anthologies curated by Judith Sonnet

SCRAPS: A Splatterpunk Horror Anthology
GASPS: A Quiet Horror Anthology

Printed in Great Britain
by Amazon